MURDER AMONG THE PINES

John Lawrence Reynolds

A
MAXINE BENSON
MYSTERY

MURDER AMONG THE PINES

ORCA BOOK PUBLISHERS

Library and Archives Canada Cataloguing in Publication

Reynolds, John Lawrence, author
Murder among the pines / John Lawrence Reynolds.
(Rapid reads)

Issued in print and electronic formats.
ISBN 978-1-4598-1819-4 (softcover).—ISBN 978-1-4598-1820-0 (pdf).—
ISBN 978-1-4598-1821-7 (epub)

I. Title. II. Series: Rapid reads
PS8585.E94M83 2018   C813'.54   C2017-904546-6
                                   C2017-904547-4

First published in the United States, 2018
Library of Congress Control Number: 2017949721

Summary: Maxine Benson, police chief in a small town, sets out to solve
the murder of her ex-husband's new girlfriend in this work of crime fiction.

*Orca Book Publishers is dedicated to preserving the environment and has
printed this book on Forest Stewardship Council® certified paper.*

Orca Book Publishers gratefully acknowledges the support for its
publishing programs provided by the following agencies: the Government
of Canada through the Canada Book Fund and the Canada Council
for the Arts, and the Province of British Columbia through
the BC Arts Council and the Book Publishing Tax Credit.

Cover photo by Creative Market/PhotoCosma
Design by Gerilee McBride

ORCA BOOK PUBLISHERS
www.orcabook.com

Printed and bound in Canada.

21 20 19 18 • 4 3 2 1

ONE

Henry Wojak turned over the top card in the deck and said, "Is this it?"

Margie glanced at the ten of clubs and said, "No, it's not." She went back to filling out the weekly arrest report for the files. It would not take long, since there had been only five arrests since Monday. Margie wanted to keep busy with it anyway. She was not impressed with Henry's card tricks.

"Is this the one?" Henry said. He took the

five of spades from the deck.

Margie swung her eyes to the card. "No, that's not it either."

"Then," Henry said, "your card must be here." He reached to the back of Margie's computer screen and withdrew the jack of hearts.

"Yes, Henry," Margie said with a sigh. "You're right. That's the card I chose. You are brilliant." She did not pretend to mean it.

"You notice the new touch I added there?" Henry said. "How I took the card from behind your computer, not out of the deck? They call that *sleight of hand*." He stroked his mustache and smiled.

"Really," Margie said.

"See, a good card trick needs to be sold," Henry said. "That takes acting skill. I used to be an actor. I was in a play once called *Harvey*. Do you know it?"

"Yes," Margie said. "I have heard of it."

"It's about a six-foot rabbit that you can't see."

"Let me guess," Margie said. "You played the rabbit."

"Very funny." Henry began to shuffle the deck.

Margie stood and walked to the coffee-maker. She had never wanted to work with a police force in the big city, where bad things happened hour by hour. And she did not want to leave Port Ainslie. What she wanted was to have more to do than watch Constable Henry Wojak show off his card tricks.

The sound of Chief Maxine Benson's car pulling into the parking lot gave her hope that something better was about to happen. Until she saw the look on Max's face.

"Hey, Chief," Henry called when Max entered the police station. "You gotta see this new trick."

"No, I don't." Max walked into her office

without a glance at Henry or Margie. When she spoke again, her voice had an edge as sharp as a razor blade. "But you need to go out on patrol," she said. "Now." She slammed her office door.

Henry put his playing cards away and left without a word. After his car pulled away, Margie poured a black coffee for Max. She carried it to the door of Max's office and went in without knocking. "Such a nice summer's day out there," Margie said.

"So I hear." Max did not lift her eyes from the papers on her desk.

"You look like you could bite off the back end of a horse." Margie set the coffee on Max's desk.

"That's how I feel."

"What's up?" Margie sat in the chair facing Max.

"My ex-husband."

"What about him?"

"You asked what's up. He is. Up from Toronto. Right here in Port Ainslie."

"How does he look?"

"What does that matter?"

Margie was about to say it seemed to matter to Max.

Before she could speak, Max frowned and said, "He looked smug."

Margie blinked. "Looked what?"

"Smug. Happy. Pleased with himself. Just plain stupid. Take your pick."

"Why don't you tell me about it?"

Max told her.

She had been cruising downtown, waving at townspeople and giving directions to tourists. Stopping her car at the crosswalk in front of the new Ainslie Inn, she smiled at people walking in front of her. Her smile faded at the sight of a man walking hand in hand with a much younger woman.

"It was him," Max said. "James Herbert

Benson. The guy I wasted twelve years of my life on."

"That's a bit harsh," Margie said.

"No, it's not. I stayed because I thought I could change him. I might as well have tried to change the color of the sky. He cheated on me every year we were married."

"Anything good to say about him?"

"He was charming. And good-looking." Max folded her arms. "Still is, damn it."

Margie nodded and said, "Ah."

"What does *ah* mean?"

"Why not tell me what happened?"

"In my marriage?"

"No, downtown. Today."

"He knew it was me driving the cruiser. So he walked up to my window, dragging this...this woman with him."

"What about her?"

"She's fifteen years younger than him. Maybe more. Long dark hair, big brown eyes, a figure like…" Max shook her head. "Never mind."

"Your classic ex-wife's nightmare," Margie said.

Max acted like she hadn't heard. "He said he wanted me to meet whatever her name is. Traffic was behind me, so I pulled into the parking lot of the inn. I got out of the car and watched her wiggle over." Max made a face like she smelled something bad. "She wiggled, he strutted."

Both her former husband and his girlfriend wore tight jeans and tighter T-shirts, Max said. The girl also wore jewelry. Lots of it. Long earrings, a charm bracelet on one arm, bangles on the other arm and a diamond ring on a silver chain around her neck. The words *Sex Goddess* were printed on her T-shirt. Her dark hair shone in the sun. Max was wearing her summer police tunic, as shapeless as a potato sack. And she was having a bad-hair day.

"He introduced us," Max said. "Told me her names. All of them. I held my hand out for her to shake. She didn't take it. She just looked at Jim and said, *You were married to her?* and giggled."

"Not very nice," Margie said. "What did your husband say to that?"

"I think he was embarrassed."

"Good. Then what?"

"I went back to the cruiser. He called out to me, but I got in and drove away."

"Now you're here and angry at him."

"No, I'm not."

"Then what are you?"

"Angry at myself. For giving a damn."

"That makes sense." Margie stood to go back to her desk. At the door she stopped, looked at Max and said, "You didn't say her name. The young woman, I mean."

"Names. She has more than one."

"Can you remember them?"

"They're burned into my jealous brain. Lana Jewel Laverne Parker."

"Lana Jewel Laverne?" Margie said. "Oh dear."

• • •

"If you can tell something about a person from her name, that one says a bunch." Geegee Gallup looked over the edge of her teacup at Max. "It sounds like her job involves taking off her clothes on a stage."

"She looks like it does too." Max sat back in her chair and stared out the window at Granite Lake. The sun was behind the hills on the far shore. The water was glass, the sky was a blue bowl over the world, and the air was calm. She loved that view. She loved her home by the lake. She loved having Geegee as a neighbor. She loved much of her life in Port Ainslie.

She hated that the sight of her ex-husband and his girlfriend had spoiled her joy.

"He was trying to make you jealous," Geegee said.

"I know."

"So he still cares for you."

"I doubt it."

"Men do dumb things where ex-wives are concerned. I know one guy who…" Geegee stopped at the sound of a car approaching. She stood to look out the window at the road. "Do you know anybody who drives a red sports car?"

Max was still staring at the lake. "No."

"How about a guy maybe six feet tall with thick dark hair and a cleft in his chin?"

Max stood and looked through the same window. "What is he doing here?" she said.

"I'll go home now," Geegee said.

Max told Geegee to wait. She walked outside and stood with her arms folded.

"Why are you here?" she asked Jim Benson as he stepped from the sports car. He had changed into a blazer and white linen shirt. Standing in the low light, he looked, Max thought, even better than he had earlier.

"I wanted to say I'm sorry," he began. "About what happened. When you saw us, Lana and me, today."

"How did you find me?"

"I asked an officer downtown, funny guy with a mustache." He meant Henry.

"He had no right to give you my address. Please leave."

"I explained that I was your husband."

"Yes. *Was*. The past tense."

Jim didn't answer. He stood looking past her at the view of the lake from her patio. "This is very nice," he said.

"It's nicer without you," Max said. "Go back to that...that *child* you brought with you. Is she your next wife?"

"She's not so bad when you get to know her," he said. "A little..." He shrugged. "Immature. We're staying at the Ainslie Inn for the weekend. Why don't you come and have a drink with us?"

"I would rather stick needles in my eyes," Max said. She turned toward her door. "Go away, or I'll lay a trespass charge on you."

"I still care," Jim said. "For you, I mean. I really do."

Max answered by slamming the door behind her.

"Now there," Geegee said as she watched Jim Benson walk back to his sports car, "is a man in love with you."

"So you heard him." Max sat in the chair facing the lake.

"Didn't have to. Saw it in his face."

"He was always a good liar," Max said.

• • •

Just after 5:00 AM, Maxine rolled across her bed to answer the telephone on the first ring. Gray predawn light seeped through her bedroom window. All calls made to the police station were routed to her phone line after hours. She knew this could only be bad news.

The woman's voice shook. "This is the night clerk at the Ainslie Inn. We have been told there's..." She began again. "There is a body in the lake. One of our guests saw it."

"Where in the lake?" Max was out of bed, one hand holding the phone to her ear.

"Near the grove of pines down the shore. I'm told it looks like..." She stopped and started over. "It looks like a young woman."

• • •

Racing toward town, Max called Henry and told him to meet her at the inn, near the pine grove. She wondered if the dead woman could be someone she had met the day before. Someone with long hair and killer legs and lots of jewelry. She told herself to stop thinking that way. It could be anyone besides Lana Jewel Laverne Parker.

Later, she felt guilty about having such a thought.

With good reason.

TWO

Max stepped from the cruiser at 5:37 AM and paused to write the time in her notebook. She had parked on a paved area near the water. Across the inlet the Ainslie Inn rose, seven stories high. The inn rarely had a vacant room on weekends. It had been a success since it opened two years earlier. Picnic tables were set among pine trees that lined a stone path leading to the inlet of the lake. During the day, many guests bought box lunches at the inn and carried them along the shore to the grove of pines, a ten-minute walk.

The sun rising behind Granite Mountain shone on the far shore of the lake. The inn was still in shadow. In the low light Max saw the body floating a little way from shore. It was easy to see the long dark hair. It was almost as easy to see that the woman was Lana Jewel Laverne Parker.

Max glanced at the people standing around her. A middle-aged man and woman in tracksuits were arm in arm, the woman's head on the man's shoulder. Max was sure they were the ones who had seen the body first and reported it to the desk clerk at the inn. Behind them stood Perry Ahenakew, a First Nations artist who had a small studio down the road. She knew him as a gentle man, a skilled artist. He nodded back at her. Not far behind him was a man named Bucky, who ran a towing service on the highway.

Near him, a white-haired man held back his dog on its leash. Behind him, a younger man in a light jacket stood shaking his head as though in sorrow.

"All of you," Max called to them. She raised an arm and pointed to the paved area where she had parked her cruiser. "This is a crime scene. Go to the parking area and wait there. Someone will talk to you later."

The group shuffled away just as Henry pulled up and parked his cruiser behind hers. "Bring a blanket with you," she called to him. "Keep these people back, and get the names of whoever called it in. Then contact the provincials in Cranston. Tell them to send the coroner." She pulled a pair of rubber gloves from her tunic, put them on and waded into the lake. She shivered as the cold water reached her waist.

The woman was floating face down. She wore a black T-shirt and jeans. When Max turned her over she could see, even in the dim light, that the victim had been beaten. She gently pulled the body toward the shore. In her years as a police officer in Toronto she had seen several dead bodies. This one did not shock her, but it made her feel guilty and sad. Guilty that she had said unkind things about the woman. Sad that her young life had been taken in such a brutal way.

She placed the body on the sand and covered it with the blanket Henry brought. She looked at people staring at the body under the blanket. At least a dozen more had joined the first group. She scanned their faces. None was her former husband's.

Henry brought a second blanket from his car for Maxine. She wrapped it around her wet legs and stood trembling in the chill of the morning air.

The sun was high enough now to shine on the gardens around the resort.

It would be another perfect summer's day. Which made it all even sadder.

• • •

The couple who had discovered the body were staying at the inn for a week. Both sat in the back of Max's police car. The wife dabbed at her eyes with a tissue as she spoke. Her husband, an arm around her shoulder, stared at the lake, biting his lip.

They had planned to walk along the shore before breakfast. "We're early risers," the woman said with a slight smile. "Up with the sun each day." Her smile faded. "I saw it..." She looked away and then back again. "I saw her as soon as we rounded the inlet, over there." She pointed down the shore. "I thought it was a bag of garbage. *Look*, I said. *Someone has tossed garbage into the water. Isn't that terrible?* Then we got closer and saw..." She shook her head.

"Was anyone else around?" Max asked.

"Nobody." She leaned toward her husband. Both looked to be in their sixties. Max saw them as beloved grandparents—mature, gentle, honest—and felt a pang of jealousy. "Dan stayed there while I went back to the inn and told them what...what we saw in the lake.

Max took their room numbers at the inn. She told them to go back to the resort. She would talk to them later if needed.

• • •

Henry had strung yellow tape to keep the growing crowd of people away from the body. Max stepped under the tape and knelt to lift a corner of the blanket. The swelling around the eyes and mouth could not hide Lana Parker's beauty. Max recalled seeing that face less than twenty-four hours earlier. She had seen the dangling gold earrings as well.

As she lowered the blanket, Max noticed that the silver chain from which the diamond ring hand hung was no longer around the woman's neck.

Do we have a robbery here? she wondered. Did this woman fight so hard to keep the chain and diamond ring that it cost her life?

Max would think about that later.

For now, all she could think about was her former husband. Where had he been when this woman was killed? And where was he now?

"Did you get something from anyone?" she asked Henry.

"Nothing," he said.

"What were they all doing here?"

"They said they were passing by and saw the old couple staring at the body and pointing. They stopped and looked. That's all. Got some names, but…" At the sound of tires on gravel, he turned to look behind him. "Here's the coroner."

• • •

Maxine liked Frank Gunn as much as anyone could like a man who spent his life looking at dead people. She said hello as he arrived. Then she stood back and let him go to work.

"Pretty clear she was drowned," Gunn said a few moments later. He stood and peeled off his rubber gloves. "Beaten first. I'll get a report to you and the other guys later."

The *other guys*, Max knew, were the Ontario Provincial Police, who had arrived just behind Gunn. When Gunn nodded at one of them, the officer walked past without speaking. He knelt near the body and began turning the pockets of Lana's jeans inside out. Max and Henry could only watch. The rules said that Max and her team were to stand aside while the OPP dealt with serious crimes. Like murder.

When Lana's body was being wheeled to the corner's van, a male voice behind Max and Henry said, "The victim carried no ID."

She turned to see an OPP officer writing in a notebook. The name on his badge said *Stanton*.

"I assume," he said without looking at her, "that you did not find any ID on the victim." He looked up at her. "Is that correct?"

"Is Stanton your first or last name?" Max said. She disliked the way OPP officers had treated her in the past. This one was treating her the same way, and she would not defer to him.

"Sergeant Gregory Stanton," he said, looking back at his notes. "I know you are Chief Maxine Benson, and you resent my taking over this case. Doesn't matter. It will happen anyway." He looked at Max. There was no smile on his face or in his voice. "I understand you knew the victim."

"I met her once," Max said. "Yesterday. For a moment."

"She live in this town?"

"She was staying at the Ainslie Inn. With her current boyfriend."

"Who is he?"

Max wanted to say, *My ex-husband.* Instead she said, "His name is James Herbert Benson. He is a former police officer. From Toronto. He and the victim were guests at the resort." She nodded toward the inn. "I assume he is in there now."

"Benson?" Stanton raised his eyebrows. "As in your last name?"

"Both of us were Toronto police officers." Max began walking to the resort. She stopped to look back at Stanton. "We'll need to speak to him, won't we?"

"It will be up to me to do that," he said. He seemed to be thinking about Max's words as he walked toward her. "Benson? Can I presume you two were married?"

"Might as well," Max said. She turned and resumed walking. "I did."

• • •

The desk clerk told them Jim Benson had not checked out of room 511. Stanton ordered the clerk not to call the room and then walked to the elevator. Max followed him. She had not been invited, but she was going anyway. Neither of them spoke on the way to the fifth floor.

When they reached room 511 Stanton knocked three times loudly on the door before it opened a little. Jim Benson looked through the opening at Max and smiled. His eyes, heavy with sleep, opened wider when he saw Stanton. It was not his eyes that Max and Stanton were staring at. It was the long row of red scratches down his neck.

Stanton pushed the door open, forcing Jim back into the room. "Are you alone?" Stanton barked. He stepped into the room, followed by Max.

"Yes, I am," Jim said. He wore a red T-shirt and boxer underwear. He looked at Max. "What's going on?"

"Where is..." Stanton looked down at his notebook. "Lana Parker?"

"I don't know." Jim sat on the edge of the unmade bed, his hands on his knees.

"When did you see her last?"

Jim looked at Max. He wanted her to ask the questions, not Stanton. When she said nothing, he said, "Last night. Around midnight." His face changed. He had, after all, been a cop. He knew where this was going. He turned to Max and said, "What's this about?"

"She's dead, Jim," Max said. "They found her floating in the lake." She nodded in the direction of the balcony doors. "Near the pine grove."

Jim stared at her for a moment. He said, "I don't believe it," and looked from Max to Gregory Stanton, shaking his head.

"Get dressed and we'll talk about it," Stanton said. He turned to Max. "I think you should leave. You have no role to play here. With the relationship between the two of you, there's a conflict of interest."

Max knew he was right. "He is not charged yet," she said, "and as a member of—" She meant to say *the local police force*.

Stanton cut her off. "All right," he said. "Sit there and listen. Just don't speak."

Fat chance, Max said to herself.

THREE

"I last saw her..."

Jim Benson slumped in a chair facing the balcony. He had put on a golf shirt and a pair of shorts. Five stories below, guests were splashing in the lake, playing tennis and volleyball, and eating breakfast. Others were walking along the shore to the pine grove, fenced with yellow tape. They wanted to see for themselves where a young woman had been found dead.

When Jim started over, his voice was flat. "I last saw her around midnight. We were..." He turned his eyes to Max and then away again. "We were getting ready for bed." He looked at a chair in the corner. Max followed his eyes and saw a black nightgown thrown across it. A short, black, sexy nightgown.

The phone had rung, Jim said, just as Lana was about to put on the nightgown. Lana practically ran to answer it. She spoke to the caller in short words—*Yes. Sure. Fine. Where? Okay.* Then she hung up, tossed the nightgown aside and told Jim she had to leave. She would be back in an hour. Maybe.

"I couldn't believe it," Jim said. "One minute we were getting ready for bed. The next minute she's back in her jeans and out the door."

"You didn't try to stop her?" Stanton said.

"Yes, I did. I wanted to know who had called and where she was going. When she

30

wouldn't tell me, I grabbed her arm. And..."
He searched for a word. "We fought a little."

"Is that how you got those scratches on
your neck?"

Jim touched them and nodded. "She
kicked me too. And punched me. Then she
ran straight out the door. No coat, no purse,
no looking back."

Max said, "Did you strike her?"

Jim looked surprised. "I would never hit
a woman."

"So she got away from you and ran off,"
Stanton said.

Jim nodded.

"What time?"

"Maybe ten after twelve."

"We can check with the hotel," Max said.
"They'll have a record of guests leaving their
rooms. And there'll be security cameras."

Stanton ignored her. "You stayed here
after she left?" he asked.

"I waited maybe an hour," Jim said. "Then I went to look for her."

"Where?"

"In and around the hotel. First the lobby and then out at the pool and the patio. I called her name. Must have called it a dozen times. If she heard me, she didn't answer."

"Did you go down the shore of the lake?"

Jim shook his head. "It was too dark. There was nobody around. I came back here to wait. I waited until after three. Then I fell asleep."

"What did you think happened to her?"

"I didn't know. It was weird. By the time I went to sleep, I didn't care. If she didn't come back by morning, I was going to check out and leave without her."

"And you wouldn't report her missing?"

Jim looked at the OPP officer. "I was a cop for fifteen years," he said. "A girl runs out in the middle of the night, doesn't come back right away? You guys wouldn't lift a finger to make a missing-person report on that for a week. So why bother?"

Stanton said nothing. Then, "We need to ask more questions. Get your things and come to Cranston with me." He looked at Max. "We don't need your permission, do we, Chief Benson?"

Max ignored him. She knew he was being sarcastic. "How did you two meet?" she asked her former husband.

"She liked my car," he said.

"Your car?" Stanton asked.

"It's a red Porsche," Max said. She turned back to her former husband. "You must be doing well."

He shrugged. "It's leased. Anyway, I parked it with the top down one day. Going to my bank in Toronto. Left the car in front of a beauty salon where she was in having a manicure. When I came out of the bank, she was standing at the curb, looking into the car. She asked if it was mine, and I said yes, all of it. She said it was sexy, and I said…" He stopped and smiled a little. "I looked at her and said if she were a car, she'd be a red Porsche like that one…"

Max looked away and said, "Oh, please."

"When was that?" Stanton asked. He seemed bored with Jim's story.

"Two weeks ago," Jim said.

"Whose idea was it to come up here?" Max asked.

Stanton stood up. "I think we can go now," he said before Jim could speak. "You two can gossip later."

"Come on, Jim," Max said. "Tell me whose idea it was to come to Port Ainslie."

"It was mine," he said. "She wanted to go somewhere for the weekend, and I picked this place. I always liked Muskoka, I heard the new resort was nice—"

"And you knew I was here," Max said.

"That wasn't a big deal," Jim said.

"Yes, it was." Max raised her voice and her anger. "You brought that piece of fluff up here—"

"Piece of fluff?"

"You wanted to show her off to me, didn't you? You wanted to prove to me that you could seduce some empty-headed sack of silicone. You were a little boy showing off your new toy, weren't you?"

"It sure seems to have made you jealous," Jim said.

"I wasn't jealous. You, on the other hand, were *pathetic!*" Max stood to shout the last word at him.

"Hey." Stanton stepped between them. He actually smiled. A little. "In case you two lovebirds forgot, we have a murder to deal with." He turned to Jim Benson. "You're a former cop. You know the score. I have questions, and I need you to answer them on video. If you want a lawyer, you can call one from Cranston, but you're not charged. Yet."

Jim said he didn't need a lawyer. Then, slipping into a light jacket, he said to Max, "Kinda like old times there for a minute, wasn't it?"

"I don't miss the fights, if that's what you mean," Max said.

"Sure you do." Jim walked to the door. "You miss it all." He looked back at her and then away.

"Make yourself useful," Stanton said to Max. "I'll send an officer up to block entry to the room. When he gets here, you go off to your office. Forensics is on its way. You know the score—don't touch a thing."

"Wait," Max said. When they stopped to look back at her, she said to Jim, "Tell me now. Did you kill her?"

"Come on, Max."

"I need to hear it. Did you or didn't you?"

Jim shook his head and waved a hand as though pushing her away. Then he and Stanton left, Stanton a step behind him.

Max closed the door and sat back in the chair. Looking around the room, she noticed a brown leather purse on a night table. She walked across the room for a closer look.

It was an expensive Roots purse with a long shoulder strap. She opened it and saw a wallet, small cosmetics bag and pink cell phone. The phone was an older model that folded closed. It turned on when Max opened it. Lana Jewel Laverne—Max couldn't help thinking of her as the woman with three names—had taken a call just before she left. Was it on this phone?

She looked at the list of calls received. The last had been from Jim, on Friday afternoon. There had been nothing since. Had Jim lied about Lana getting a phone call around midnight? If he had lied about that, what else had he lied about?

Max felt her heart sink. Though happy to be free of her marriage, she still felt a need to protect her former husband.

From the list of calls received on the pink phone she went to calls sent. One had been made at 6:03 PM the previous day and had lasted less than a minute. Max wrote the name and the Toronto phone number in her notebook—*Martin Zeyer*. She scrolled back to write the names of other callers and their numbers from the past two days.

She knew she should turn the list over to the OPP, but the Forenics team would find the phone anyway. And besides, they wouldn't even need the phone to track her calls. They could get all they needed from the phone service. She replaced the phone in the purse just as someone knocked on the door. "It's all yours," she said when she opened the door to the OPP officer. Then she added as she left, "You know the score. Don't you dare touch a thing."

She couldn't resist it.

FOUR

"What will the OPP tell you about the case?" Margie asked.

It was almost noon. Max handed her notes to Margie, who would send them to the OPP in Cranston. Her notes did not include the names copied from Lana Parker's phone.

"Not much," Max said. Margie had brought her tea and cookies for lunch. Henry was at the Ainslie Inn, helping to keep onlookers away from the crime scene.

"They're the ones who handle murders. Plus, I have a personal link with Jim. There was no way for me be involved."

"Could he do it?" Margie asked. "Murder someone that way?"

Max sat in silence. Then she said, "No. Yes. Maybe."

"That clears things up," Margie said.

"The thing is..." Max paused and closed her eyes. She had tried not to think about her former husband being guilty of murder. It wasn't working. She started again. "This was a crime of passion. But they met just two weeks ago. Even Jim admitted it wasn't serious. Not that it matters. He had flings all through our marriage. None of them were serious either."

"And he still cares for you."

Max shrugged. "I think he brought the girl up here to make me jealous. He wrote me letters for months after our divorce, saying he was sorry."

"Is he an angry man?"

"Not angry enough to kill anyone. He used to say he was a lover, not a fighter. Well, he got that right. It's what ruined our marriage. People used to smile and say, *Everybody loves Jim.* When I heard that I'd say, *Yeah, that's the trouble.*" She shook her head. "I can't see him getting angry enough to kill anyone."

"Men can get weird over the strangest things," Margie said. "My son Robbie gave his girlfriend a bracelet when he was just out of college. It cost him a month's salary. A week later she told him she wanted to date other boys. Robbie couldn't believe it. When he asked for the bracelet back, she told him she was keeping it."

Margie heaved a sigh. "I could not believe the way he acted about it. He cried, he shouted, he broke a window, he phoned her over and over." She shook her head. "He was not my Robbie anymore. Not my sweet, quiet Robbie. I'm not saying your former husband couldn't do what the officers in Cranston think he did. Just that some men can't help themselves when a woman changes her mind. Maybe that's what happened with your ex." She stood to leave.

"How did things work out with your son?" Max said.

"Fine," Margie said. "They made up in a month and got married that fall. Gave me two lovely grandchildren, and there's another on the way."

• • •

After lunch Max drove to the Ainslie Inn to meet Henry. The area along the shore was still fenced with yellow tape. Two OPP cruisers were parked near the grove of pines. Another was in the resort parking lot. Some people stood in groups, speaking in low tones.

Murder in a place like Port Ainslie? they seemed to be saying. *Impossible.*

Others acted as though it was just another summer's day in Muskoka. They swam, they played, they shopped, they laughed, they took selfies. Life, Max told herself, goes on. She sent Henry back to the station and walked through the inn's lobby to the office of Pamela Rosart, the resort manager. They needed to talk.

• • •

"The police have taken over," Pam Rosart said. She and Max were seated in chairs in Pam's office. Pam meant the OPP, which seemed to be everywhere on the property. "I know this is a serious crime, but it's not my inn to run anymore."

Max and Pam had met when the Ainslie Inn opened. From Prince Edward Island, Pam used a friendly tone to hide her sometimes stern approach to life and business. Like Max, she felt the need to prove herself as a woman in charge. But she also, like Max, let herself see the humor in life whenever it appeared.

"It's going to be a few rough days for you," Max said.

"It's breaking up the routine. But you know what? I was enjoying the routine."

"Have any guests checked out because of the body being found?"

"Maybe just two or three. The suits at head office are upset anyway. They're afraid news of the murder will stop guests from coming here, but I doubt it." She leaned toward Max and dropped her voice. "Was that really your ex-husband who was staying here with her?"

Max nodded, saying nothing.

Pam sat back. "I heard they took him to Cranston. Why would they do that?"

"They want to ask him questions," Max said. "I doubt they'll be laying charges."

"They're tearing that room apart up there," she said. She meant room 511. "We had to move guests off the floor. The officers are giving orders to everybody they see. I think they're acting like jerks."

"Some cops like to throw their weight around," Max said. She stood to leave. "Call me if they cause too much trouble. I might be able to make it easier for you."

Leaving Pam Rosart's office, she walked across the lobby. Two OPP officers watched as she approached.

"How are you, officers?" Max said as she passed.

"Just fine, Chief," one of them said. They were both smiling.

Max told herself they weren't being sarcastic. She went back to the station and stayed there the rest of the day.

• • •

Geegee had invited Maxine to share a glass of wine and smoked oysters with her that evening. She also, Maxine knew, wanted to hear as much as Max was willing to tell about Lana Parker's murder. Geegee's husband, Cliff, was playing guitar at a sunset concert in the park.

They sat in Geegee's living room with its view of the sun hanging low over Granite Lake. It was another splendid summer night in Muskoka. The sight reminded her why she had moved there. She might regret some of the decisions she'd made in her life—like marrying Jim Benson—but she would never regret moving to Muskoka.

Max rarely drank alcohol, even a half glass of something weak like the Pinot Grigio she was sipping now. She never knew when she might be called to deal with trouble somewhere in town. Having alcohol on her breath at a crime site would be a problem. But she made an exception tonight. Maxine needed to share her feelings with someone she could trust, someone other than Margie or Henry. They would judge her if she showed weakness or made any missteps. Geegee would not.

"So the OPP is talking to your husband…" Geegee said.

"Ex-husband."

"You kept his last name."

"I was too lazy to change it. Plus, it's the name I've used all through my police career." Max saw Geegee's eyebrows rise halfway up her forehead. "That does not mean I wanted to stay married to him."

"Okay," said Geegee. "So how come you're worried he may be charged with murder? And don't say you're not. It's all over your face."

"He and I have a past," Max said. "It wasn't always good, but it's like…" She looked out at the setting sun for an answer. "Like an old pair of jeans you own that are torn or too tight.

You should throw them out, but you can't. Every time you look at them, you remember how happy you were when you wore them."

"That," Geegee said, "is the worst excuse I've heard since the one about the dog eating your homework."

"Yeah, well." Max smiled and then said, "There's always the risk that he could be found guilty. Police officers know this can happen. We see it both ways. Bad guys go free, good guys get the shaft."

Geegee leaned toward Max. "They took him to Cranston just to ask a few things, right?"

Max knew where this was going. "That's all. Just get some facts down for the record." Cliff Gallup's car pulled into the driveway. She watched him step from the car and walk to the door.

"So you don't think they'll charge him with murder?"

Max carefully set her glass aside and stood to leave. "No," she said. "I don't expect they will. Hi, Cliff." She thanked Geegee for the wine, gave Cliff a quick kiss on the cheek as he came into the room and walked back to her house.

• • •

Max did not believe in psychics. She did believe in instincts, however. When her telephone rang just as she was getting ready for bed two hours later, her instincts told her it would be bad news.

"It's me, Jim," the shaking voice on the phone said. "They're charging me."

"With what?" She didn't actually need to ask.

"Murder. First degree. If I confess, they might make it second degree."

"Do you have a lawyer?"

"I will in the morning. Look, Max, you know I did not do this."

"Just a minute." She reached for her notebook and opened it. "Do you know a man named Zeyer?"

"Don't think so. Why?"

Max almost told him she had taken Zeyer's name from Lana's cell phone. Then she remembered that police had been known to listen to phone calls from jail. "Just someone who knows Margie," she lied. "He asked about you. How are you doing?"

"Margie? Who's Margie?"

"Never mind."

"You know they're locking me up here, right?"

"That's what they do with accused murderers, Jim." Max didn't get as much enjoyment from saying this as she had hoped.

"I need you to help me."

"I'll drive down tomorrow."

"Max," he said, "I need more than that."

She hung up without saying goodbye.

It took a very long time for her to fall asleep.

FIVE

The next morning Max's head felt as though it were stuffed with wool. Old, scratchy, itchy wool. Arriving at the station late, she handed Margie the list of names copied from Lana's phone. "Call Toronto Police and ask for any criminal records on these names. Photos would be good too. Tell them we're looking into something here in town. Don't say it's about the murder."

She reached for one of Margie's oatmeal

cookies. It would be her breakfast on the drive to Cranston. "Where's Henry?"

"On patrol," Margie said. She was frowning at the list. "Downtown near the inn. I thought it would look good to have him there. He called to say four or five OPP teams are still there. They won't tell him a thing except to get lost. Where did you get these names?"

"Would you believe they're my old boyfriends?" She headed for the door. "I'm off to Cranston. To see the OPP. Should be back in two, maybe three hours."

"Maxine?"

Max stopped at the door and turned.

Margie's voice had changed. "Don't take any crap from those guys."

• • •

"This is a courtesy," Sergeant Gregory Stanton said. He was leading Max down a hall toward the holding cells in the regional OPP building. "I'm very busy dealing with this case. I could easily send you back where you came from. You know that."

"I also know," Max said, looking straight ahead, "that the crime occurred in my jurisdiction. So I have a right to hear basic facts. And he is allowed visits. Whether by another law officer or an ex-wife, it does not matter."

"We can withdraw that right at any time," Stanton said. He did not look at her. "For any reason."

"You do that," Max said, smiling, "and I'll have six judges come down on you like a ton of bricks."

"I have been assigned control over this case," Stanton said. "I don't think I need to remind you that it concerns a murder."

"Which took place in my area of command."

"You will have access to reports. Nothing else."

"I am here to be updated."

Stanton said, "I don't need to remind you that you are required to share with us any facts you might come up with." Neither had looked at the other since they began walking.

Max wanted to say, *Then don't bother reminding me*, but she kept quiet.

"We, on the other hand, don't have to share certain facts with you," Stanton said to her. "Unless we choose to." He pushed on a heavy door. It opened into a room with three large glass panels. In front of each panel were a stool and a telephone.

Jim Benson sat on the other side of the middle panel, his hands folded in front of him. At the sight of Max a small smile appeared on his face. He picked up the telephone when Max sat down. Max reached for the phone on her side of the panel and sat staring at Stanton until he left the room.

"Thanks," Jim said.

He began to say more, but Max cut him off. "Have you met your lawyer?"

"She just left."

"Is she cute?"

Jim frowned. "What?"

"Is she cute? That's how you judge women. Do they have a nice butt? Have they got big—"

"Max!" He spoke so loud, she didn't need the telephone to hear him. "I'm facing a charge of murder here. How can you—"

She cut him off again. "Relax. I don't believe you did it. I just can't quite forgive you for all the things you did in our marriage."

"What does that have to do with my being charged with murder?"

"Nothing. It just seemed a good time to say it. Are you still telling them that Lana left after taking a phone call in your room?"

He nodded. "Of course I am."

"On what phone? Hers or the inn's?"

"The inn's, I think."

"You *think*?"

"I was distracted. We were..." He bit his lip and started over. "She'd been teasing me all day and...anyway, when she got the call and said she was leaving, I guess I lost it. Okay?" His words seemed to make him stronger and a bit defiant. "Okay?"

Maxine sat thinking for a moment. Then she said, "When I saw both of you downtown, she wore a chain around her neck with a ring on it. A diamond ring."

"What about it?"

Max was about to tell him it was gone from Lana's body. The police will be listening to us, she reminded herself. So she said, "It looked like a nice ring."

She watched Jim's expression change. He nodded in understanding, and his voice became more formal. "It was a very nice ring," he said. He was almost too careful with his words. "Big stone. Said it was two carats. Mounted in platinum. From Bentley's."

"Bentley's? Is that the new store trying to outdo Tiffany's?"

"So I hear."

"Must have cost a fortune."

"So I hear," Jim repeated in the same tone.

"Where'd she get it?"

"A friend. That's all she told me. I didn't care. She made a big deal of showing it to me and saying a friend had bought it for her."

"Must have been a special friend."

Jim grunted.

"She might have been killed for a ring like that," Maxine said.

"I was thinking the same thing."

"Robbery's a good motive."

"I may point that out to my lawyer."

"You might also tell her..." Max heard a

door open behind her. On the other side of the glass, Jim looked past her and scowled.

"This visit is over." Max turned to see Sergeant Stanton reaching for the telephone in her hand. On the other side of the glass an officer was pulling Jim to his feet.

"This," Max said standing up, "is not right."

Stanton took the telephone from her. "Neither is passing info to a suspect."

"I was not passing anything to him."

"You did when you suggested something was missing from the victim's body."

"I did no such thing."

"That's not what I heard."

"You had no right to be listening."

"So launch a complaint."

"I'll get a court order."

"Yeah, yeah, yeah." Stanton turned off the light and held the door open. "Tell you what. On your way to see the judge, step into room five down the hall. I'll bring you a coffee, if you like. How do you take it?"

"Black," Max said as she walked past him. "No hemlock."

• • •

Room five was small and gray, furnished with a table and two chairs. A video screen hung from the wall above the table. Stanton had brought two paper cups of coffee and some sheets of paper into the room. He set one coffee cup on the table in front of Maxine and slid a sheet of paper across to her. "Read this," he said. "It's a record of the telephone calls coming into the Ainslie Inn on Saturday night. From six in the evening until two in the morning." He tapped the papers with a finger. "No call was made to room 511."

He slid another sheet to her. "This is a list of calls to the victim's cell phone for the same period. No calls there either. Yet your former spouse tells us she took a call just after midnight. He can't be sure from which phone. She hangs up and they have a quarrel—a fight, really—and she walks out. He tells us she was on her way to meet whoever called her. But no one called her that night, either in the room or on her cell. By the way, we found tissue under her fingernails. It's being checked for DNA. Guess whose we expect it to be?"

Max didn't need to hear more. She began to stand.

Stanton held up a hand to stop her. "Before you go," he said, "let's watch a movie."

He pressed a button on the video. When the screen lit up, Max was looking at an overhead view of the Ainslie Inn's lobby. The date and time appeared—12:18:02 AM Sunday. Most of the people on the screen were walking left to right across the lobby, toward the elevators.

After a moment the slim figure of a young woman appeared walking from right to left. Her dark hair swung as she crossed the lobby. She was wearing tight jeans and a T-shirt.

"This is from the lobby security camera," Stanton said. "That's Parker."

Max watched Lana pass a bank of telephones on her way to the lakeside exit of the inn.

The screen went blank. When it lit again the time read 12:53:18 AM. Almost no one was in the lobby. Within a few moments Jim Benson entered on the right of the picture, taking the same route as Lana Parker. He moved slowly, as though unsure where to go. Standing at the windows overlooking the lake, he checked his watch. Then he walked out of the lobby toward the lakeside exit.

"You know who that is," Stanton said. "Now watch closely."

Again the screen went dark before the same view appeared again. The time was now 1:17:23 AM. No one could be seen in the lobby until Jim Benson walked across the screen from left to right. His walk had changed. He did not look unsure of himself now. Taking long strides, he headed straight for the elevators.

Stanton turned off the video. "Your spouse lied about a telephone call coming for Parker at midnight," he said. "There was no call. We think he found her outside, sitting by the lake. When she refused to come back to the room, they fought. He lost his temper and killed her. She died from drowning, by the way. The coroner confirmed it. Beaten around the head and then held under water until she was dead. That's likely when the chain broke and the ring fell into the water. The one you talked about." He leaned toward Max. "Held her under until she died. How does that make you feel?"

Max rose and walked to the door. "Ex," she said. She opened the door and strode out to the hall.

"Ex-what?" Stanton called after her.

"Ex-spouse."

She walked out of the building, got into her cruiser and spun the tires as she left. She broke the speed limit all the way to Port Ainslie.

SIX

Back in her office, Max sat and thought about her career. And about her ex-husband.

In some ways, being chief of police in Port Ainslie was all she had hoped it would be. Her work did not make demands on either her time or her training. Most of the job involved being visible to residents and keeping an eye out for trouble. At times she felt more like a high school teacher than a police chief.

True, she had plenty of time to relax at

her home by the lake. But she wanted to do more than relax. She wanted to do other things. Big things, like solving murders. Yet murder was not on her duty list. She had agreed that serious crimes in and around Port Ainslie would be handled by the OPP. But how could she do nothing when someone had been murdered in her own town?

There was more to it, of course. The arrest of her former husband on a charge of first-degree murder meant she must stand aside. And the OPP had a good record for solving murder cases. She just hated not being part of it.

Of course, she did not believe Jim Benson was guilty. Even though he had been known to tell lies. Why, if Maxine had a dollar for every lie he had told her when they were married...

She went back to dealing with the question of his guilt.

Had Jim lied when he said Lana Jewel Laverne Parker left their room after getting a telephone call? There was no record of a call on her cell phone at that time. And no record of a call to the room. He must have lied. And if he had lied about that, what else had he lied about?

She recalled the security video of Jim walking through the lobby. He said he had been looking for Lana Parker. He also said he hadn't found her. But what if he had found her alone near the pine grove? What if the fight in their room had started over again, and he'd killed her? He'd had time to do it. And if she had his DNA under her nails...

Max reminded herself she no longer loved her former husband. But they still had a past. They would always share that past, and she would always feel some concern for him.

She asked herself what she would do if the case were hers to solve and Jim Benson were not her former husband. Would she suspect him? She knew the answer. She would believe he was guilty and set out to prove it. She would try to put him in prison for a very long time.

"You might as well go home."

Margie's soft voice pulled Max away from her thoughts. It was late in the day. She could do some work on the porch of her home, looking over the lake. There was always paperwork to be finished. And things to consider.

"You could use an hour or two on your own," Margie said. "I can tell. Nothing is going to happen here. Henry is downtown, keeping a watch on things. And you can start all over again in the morning. Things will work out. They always do."

• • •

Cliff and Geegee talked Max into joining them for dinner that night. Cliff had picked up some steaks for the barbecue. Geegee made a good potato salad, and Max brought a bottle of Merlot to share.

They ate on the patio with the sun low over the lake. A weak breeze bothered the trees, and a loon called from the far shore. The steaks were perfect, the salad was great, and the Merlot tasted so good that Max agreed to have another glass. She didn't care this time that she might be called on for police work. Let the OPP do it if they want. This is why I am here, Max told herself, looking around. This is why I wanted this job. This makes it all worthwhile.

Cliff and Geegee rarely asked Max about her work. They knew she had to keep details hidden, and they respected that. But now, sitting with them in the warm evening air, Max felt a strong need to talk about Lana Parker's death. Cliff and Geegee knew Jim had been charged with the murder. Everyone did.

All the TV channels had carried the story. It was big news in Toronto. An ex-cop from the big city charged with murder? The papers would be all over it.

She told Cliff and Geegee some basics, little more than the news channels had reported. "I don't believe Jim did it," she said when she finished. Then she shrugged. "There's nothing I can do to prove it. But I can see why he has been charged. It's complex. Very complex."

"Funny," Cliff said. "I had a student tell me today that he was going to give up trying to play the guitar. He said it was too complex for him. *All them fingers on the strings*, he said." Cliff's voice rose in pitch. He talked like an annoyed teenager. "*I can't keep track of them. How do you do that?*" Cliff smiled and shook his head. "I told him to make it simple. *Find a shortcut*, I said. He asked how, and I told him to look for a shorter string. What I meant was, he needed to find another way to play the same note on a closer string. I call it a shorter string. You find a shorter string, and you can get to the note easier."

Cliff was trying to help by talking about what he knew best, which was guitars. Max knew little more about guitars than that they had strings. Guitars had nothing to do with keeping law and order. Or solving murders.

Geegee changed the subject to all the garden work she had done that day. Cliff said he planned to paint the garage door brown. Geegee said it should stay white. Cliff said what they really needed was a new door. Max finished her coffee, thanked them both and went home.

Hours later, lying in bed waiting to fall asleep, Max remembered Cliff's words. Not the ones about garage doors. The ones about finding a shorter string when playing a guitar. She needed a shorter string to explain the telephone call that Jim said had come to their room in the inn. Was there something to explain Jim's story about a phone call that the police said never happened?

She woke sometime after 3:00 AM. She may have seen a shorter string after all. And she knew exactly where.

SEVEN

Max called Pam Rosart before leaving home in the morning. It was going to be one of those glorious summer days that seemed made for Muskoka. At the Ainslie Inn she found Pam waiting at the entrance. When she asked, "What's up?" Max said, "Follow me." She walked in to the inn, through the main doors, past the reception desk and pointed to the bank of telephones against the wall. "What are those?" she asked.

Pam folded her arms and rolled her eyes. "A mistake."

"House phones?"

"Yes," Pam said. "When I saw the plans, I told the company to forget about them. Nobody uses house phones in hotels anymore. But they were in the budget, and some people can't break old habits, so..."

"Can somebody call a room here in the inn from one of them?"

"That's what they're for."

"If they did, the call would not go through the switchboard, right?"

"No, they're just—" Pam began.

"So it's a shortcut past the switchboard. To reach somebody registered here in the inn."

"That's one way of putting it. What are you thinking?"

"I'm thinking I'd like to watch a video."

• • •

Pam led Max to the security room next to her office. "We made copies of the videos for the OPP," she said. She sat at a small control panel. "We kept the originals." She began pressing buttons.

"How many security cameras do you have?" Maxine asked.

"It depends." Pam moved a lever, and the screen lit up.

"Depends on what?"

"Some systems are portable. We move them around as we need them."

"Why move them around?"

Pam smiled tightly. "People get to know where they are. And where they are not. They learn how to avoid the cameras. Both our staff and guests. We move the portables now and then so you can never be sure if you're being watched. They can be anywhere in the resort at any time." She turned a switch and pushed some buttons. "Here's what the lobby camera saw." The screen came alive to show the lobby of the inn. The date and time said it had been recorded at 10:00:00 PM Saturday night. "This is what we gave the OPP. The camera's fixed and covers the whole area, but I can't zoom with it." She entered another date and time. "You've seen this, right?"

"Don't show me the girl and Jim," Maxine said. "Show me the lobby starting at midnight."

Pam pushed more buttons until the time said *12:00:00* Sunday morning. In an upper corner of the screen was the bank of house phones. No one was using them.

The women watched people walk across the lobby. An elderly man and woman shuffled past. When the man stopped to speak, the woman nodded and rested her head against him for a moment. Then they set off for the elevator again. Two young women crossed the lobby. One spoke and they both giggled as they walked. Others passed the camera. All looked weary from a day in the sun. There is nothing here to see, Max told herself.

And there wasn't. Until the screen read *12:06:17.*

That's when a man entered the screen from the left. Too far from the camera to be seen in detail, he was wearing a T-shirt and athletic shorts. Max guessed he was in his late twenties, maybe early thirties. He walked straight to the house phones, picked up a receiver and punched in three numbers. Max was sure they were 5-1-1.

"What time did the OPP ask you to start the video?" she asked.

"They said from 12:10." Pam's eyes had not left the video image.

"Are calls made from house phones recorded?"

"No. The phones are on their own system."

At 12:06:56 the man hung up the phone. His hands in his pockets, he stood looking around the lobby. Then he turned and walked across the lobby to the lakeside door.

"That's the phone call to room 511," Max said. "That's why it didn't show up on the computer."

"If they had asked me—the police," Pam said, "we could have started the video earlier and seen him."

"They didn't ask," Max said, "because they didn't want to know. They thought they had their man."

Pam nodded at the video screen. "Who was that man on the phone?"

"I don't know," Max said. "But something about him is familiar."

When Pam asked if she should tell the OPP what they had found, Maxine said she would handle it. In her own way.

. . .

Max could tell nothing about the man who had used the house phone beyond guesses of his height and his age. Had she seen him before? She wasn't sure. He could be any of thousands of young men who arrived in Muskoka on midsummer weekends.

On her way back to the station, she thought about telling the OPP what she had found. She would say that someone had used a house phone to call a room in the inn, and there was no record of the call. It had been made around the time Jim Benson claimed Lana had received a call. They would ask her to tell them which room the man had dialed. She would say it looked like 511. *Looked like?* they would say with a laugh. They would ask if she could prove it was room 511. She would say no. They would ask if she could identify this man who made a phone call.

Again she would have to say no. And they would laugh at her again.

She did not want anyone laughing at her. More than anything, she did not want a macho OPP homicide cop laughing at her. So she wouldn't call them. Not yet, anyway.

• • •

"Where's Henry?" Maxine asked when she arrived at the police station.

Margie looked up from her crossword. "Down on Main Street," she said. "Bop Chadwick's been trying to sell some junk to tourists."

Bruce Olivier Pratt Chadwick, or Bop (no one had called him Bruce since high school), had grown up in Port Ainslie. When Bop's parents sent him off to college, he came back with no diploma but with a pregnant young wife. He and his family moved to Toronto after the baby arrived. Some years later Bop returned without wife, child, job or future. Even his parents were gone, his mother from cancer and his father from a broken heart. This had happened more than ten years ago. Now all Bop had was an endless taste for alcohol.

People in town liked Bop. Many gave him food, shelter and sometimes money for a bottle of cheap wine. Whenever Bop became a problem, Max or Henry would bring him in. A pot of hot coffee, a night in cell number two and Margie's scrambled eggs and onions in the morning made him a new man. Or at least a sober one, and Bop would teeter off to a nearby park bench. On cold nights with nowhere to sleep, Bop would often wander in on his own and claim to have committed some otherwise unknown crime. Margie or Henry would put him in cell number two—it had a window facing the lake—and wake him in the morning.

Max headed for her office.

"And those reports came in," Margie called after her.

"What reports?"

"On the names you got from that poor girl's phone." Margie followed her and handed Max several sheets of paper.

"Thanks." Max carried them to her desk and began turning the pages.

There were five in all, listed by their last names and in alphabetical order. All were Toronto residents. The first was a woman named Kim Allen, who worked at a hair salon on Jarvis Street. The next two names belonged to men. One worked as a tailor on Queen Street, the other in a high-priced shoe store on Bloor Street. The fourth, another woman, lived in Kingston. None of those four had a police record.

But the man on the last page did. In fact, he had much more than that.

His name was Zeyer. The police knew of him. Based on his rap sheet, they knew him very well. Martin Yuri Zeyer was thirty-one years old. At age sixteen he had been charged with car theft. Later he faced three charges of assault on women and was found guilty of dealing drugs. By age twenty-eight he had served two terms in jail, one for six months and the other for two years.

Subject remains active in narcotics trade, the report said. *Lives well, claims to work as mechanic for source of income.* Zeyer's home address was given as Sparky's Cycle Works, a known hangout for Toronto drug dealers.

Max turned the page. At the sight of the face staring back at her, she gasped so loudly that Margie called out, "You all right in there?"

To Max, Martin Yuri Zeyer's narrow eyes, curly hair and cold smile added up to a man who could attract some women with a wink and a wave of his hand.

It was also a face Max had seen recently. She had seen it as he stood near the grove of pines, watching Lana Parker's body floating in the water. And she was sure it was the man on the video, calling room 511 from a house phone in the lobby of the Ainslie Inn.

EIGHT

More than anything else, Maxine wanted to be a good cop, which meant doing the right thing. The right thing to do now was to share everything she knew about the murder of Lana Parker with OPP Sergeant Stanton. To not report what she knew would mean concealing evidence.

She called the OPP office in Cranston, fearing they would mock her.

She was right.

"So let me get this straight," Stanton said. "You've got a guy using the house phones at the inn. But you don't know who he called. Or what he said. You think you saw him at the scene when the body was found, but you can't swear it in court. Have I got this right so far?"

"He has a record for assault," Max said. "On women."

"Can you connect him with the victim?"

"No. Not yet."

"Not yet? When?"

"I don't know."

"You don't know." Stanton's sarcasm was thick and heavy. "Are you leaving anything out?"

"Like what?"

"Like having a good reason to call me about this?"

"Look, Sergeant—" Max began.

Stanton cut her off. "No, *you* look, Ms. Chief of Police. If you have feelings for

your ex-husband, good for you. And good for
him. But trying to pull us off his case with
dumb hunches like this won't work. We don't
use hunches. We don't *need* them. We have
a video of Jim Benson following the victim.
We have his DNA under her fingernails.
We have matching scratches on the suspect's
neck. Do you have anything like that?"

Before Max could speak, Stanton went on.
"He killed that woman, and we're going to
prove he did. So don't bother us with hunches,
all right? If you get something we can take to
trial, call me and I'll listen. Until then, go back
to traffic duty in your little burg and leave
serious stuff to us." And he hung up.

• • •

"Henry's on his way," Margie said after Max
hung up from her call to Stanton. She set a
mug of tea on Max's desk. "Bringing in Bop

Chadwick. How'd you do with your call?"

"I was told to stick to traffic duty. They think I'm trying to weaken their case against Jim." She picked up the photo of Martin Zeyer. "I know this man was there when we recovered the body. I saw him, just for a second..."

"For a second? In the dawn light?" Margie shook her head. "A good lawyer would tear that apart." Margie turned to look out the window. "Here comes Henry with Bop. Poor soul looks a mess." She meant Bop.

Max followed Margie out to the office when Henry arrived. He was holding Bop by the elbow.

"Mornin', Margie," Bop said. "Henry tells me you got a batch of butter tarts." He turned to Max. "Mornin', Chief."

Bop wore loud plaid shorts, plastic sandals and a yellow T-shirt with *Westdale Warriors* printed in green on the front. It wasn't his clothes that caught Max's eye, however. It was the silver chain that dangled from one of his hands. "Where did you get that?" she said and reached for it.

Bop pulled his hand back. "I didn't steal it," he said, looking hurt. "I'm no thief. You know that."

"Let me see it," Max said, and Bop handed it to her.

"Was trying to sell it downtown," Henry said. "No takers. It's broken."

Max could see that the clasp was closed. Someone had snapped the chain by pulling it apart. "Where did you get this?" she asked.

"Found it," Bop said. "Down by the lake. Across from the inn."

"In the pine trees?"

Bop nodded. "Under a picnic table. See, I was sleepin' there last night. On the table. Opened my eyes this mornin', looked down and saw somethin' shining. Most of it was under some old leaves." He lowered his voice. "What do you think it's worth?"

"It's a treasure."

"Yeah? Really?" Bop held out his hand. "I'll settle for five bucks."

Max was walking back to her office. "Margie, pour Bop some tea and give him a couple of butter tarts. I've got some thinking to do."

• • •

"This is the chain I saw around the victim's neck," Max said to Henry a few minutes later. The broken chain lay on her desk. "I'm sure of it." She slid the photo of Martin Zeyer to him. "And this is the man—"

"Who was there when we arrived." Henry pulled the photo closer. "He was standing behind Perry Ahenakew and Bucky what's his name, the tow-truck guy. He wouldn't look at me." Henry tapped the photo with his finger. "When I started taking names, he was gone. Didn't matter. He was just an onlooker."

"He was more than that." Max nodded as she spoke. "He was a murderer. And still is."

• • •

Max told Henry about the video showing the man using a house phone at the resort. Margie stood in the open doorway, listening.

"Stanton isn't buying it," Max said. She held up the broken chain. "He won't buy this either. I can't swear this was the chain around the victim's neck. No court would believe me."

"So why is it important?" Henry asked.

"Because I know Jim Benson did not kill that woman," Max said. "What would be the motive for someone else to kill her? It wasn't sex. And she knew nobody else here that we know of. So it had to be robbery."

"You said there was a ring on the chain," Margie said.

"A big one," Max said. "Big enough for someone to kill for it." She looked at Henry. "Get Bop to show you where he found this chain. Line it up with the location of the body. Then follow the line, looking for the ring. Rake the sand. Look under leaves."

"That's all?" Henry said. "We don't get a team, maybe one of those things that finds stuff under ground?"

Max shook her head. "Not yet."

Henry shrugged. "Come on, Bop," he said as he left her office. "We're on a treasure hunt. Bring one of those tarts with you."

"Not much chance of finding the ring that way," Margie said when Henry and Bop were gone.

"It's worth a look," Max said.

"Someone else may have found it by now."

"Maybe. But I don't think so." Max picked up the photo of Zeyer. "If this guy is the killer, why did he hang around until morning? She was dead shortly after midnight." She looked at Margie. "We don't know why he murdered that poor girl. But he did it in the dark of night. So why was he still there when the sun was coming up?"

"To look for something." Margie smiled and nodded. "Probably the ring. Because it was worth a lot of money."

"More than that," Max said. "I think it was because the ring could be traced back to him. The victim told Jim someone had given it to her a couple of weeks ago. I remember that ring. You couldn't miss it. We would be able to trace a ring like that and maybe put him at the scene of the murder." She held the chain up for Margie. "This snapped when it was yanked off the victim's neck. Pulled hard, in anger. The same anger that I think made him kill her. Then he went looking for the ring."

"That's why he was still hanging around when you got there."

"It was getting light. The sun was up. He couldn't find it in the dark."

"So maybe he bought it for her. Paid a lot of money and wanted it back."

"Or maybe for more than the money. Maybe for what it might tell us about him. Jim said the ring was from Bentley's. Whoever bought it for her paid a lot of money. And if he bought it new, there would be a record of the sale."

"Do you think Henry will come back with the ring?"

"I doubt it."

"So why send him and Bop to look for it?"

"To give me time to think about what to do next."

"I can take a hint," Margie said, and she closed the door behind her.

Maxine began by phoning Pam Rosart at the Ainslie Inn to ask another favor. Then she called out to Margie, "How do you think Henry would feel about shaving off his mustache?"

NINE

Sparky's Cycle Works was in two buildings in east Toronto. One, all white brick and chrome, displayed new motorcycles through its plate-glass windows. The other was an old frame building next door. A faded sign over its door said *Sparky's Repairs*. Instead of chrome and tiles, it had worn wood floors covered with tools and grease.

Arnie Sparks had launched Sparky's more than forty years earlier. It had become a favorite of outlaw motorcycle gangs in the city. Sparks was good at fixing things but not at running a business. Almost broke, he had sold the part of the business that handled new bikes and kept the service and repair side to pay his debts.

Martin Zeyer was often in the repair shop, but not as a mechanic. He paid Sparky to let him be there. This let him claim he had a job at Sparky's, which explained his income. Zeyer also paid for the use of a telephone in Sparky's repair shop. Zeyer had his own cell phone, but it was for friends. The shop phone was for business.

It was his cell phone that rang the next morning when Martin Zeyer was leaning against a work bench, sipping coffee. Zeyer set aside his cup and answered in his usual way. "Who's this?"

The man on the other end sounded drunk. Or sleepy. Zeyer couldn't be sure which.

"Hey, yeah," he said. "I'm trying to reach a guy named Zeyer, see."

"Who are you?" Zeyer didn't know the voice, and he didn't trust anyone he didn't already know.

"Okay, okay. See, my name is Casey, Hank Casey. Is this Zeyer? You don't know me, but—"

"Damn right I don't know you. What do you want? Make it quick—I'm a busy guy."

"Yeah, I figured that. Busy making all that money."

Zeyer's face grew hard. "What money?"

"Whatever it took to buy this ring. I figure ten, maybe twelve thousand retail, right? Am I close?"

Zeyer looked around to make sure no one was nearby. He lowered his voice. "I don't know anything about any ring."

"Sure you do. I'm looking at it now. Standard cut, about two carats, looks like

VVS2 clarity, platinum Bentley's mount. Good taste you got. Or maybe it was your girlfriend's."

"So you found some ring. What makes you think it's mine?"

"The laser etching."

"The what?"

"You don't know about that? Most people don't. See, I used to be a jeweler. Good one too. But I got greedy, fenced some goods to get drugs. So I got caught. Did time and now nobody will hire me. Now I'm up here cutting grass at the Ainslie Inn. I spend a lot of time looking at stuff. Mostly stuff on the ground."

"What's that—" Zeyer began.

The caller kept talking. "See, good stones like this one, they get lasered. Cut a code into the bottom of the stone. So's they can be traced. The insurance people like it. And I still got some friends in the business. So I put it under my loupe—"

"Your what?"

"My glass for getting a close look at stones. Only thing I kept from my jewelry business. So I use it to read the code, call it in to Bentley's, and they tell me it's yours. Or used to be. The ring, I mean. I got a chain too. Did she wear this ring around her neck on it? The chain, I mean? Would've looked better on her finger."

Zeyer took a deep breath. "How'd you find me?"

"Not a whole bunch of Zeyers in the book. What is that, your name? Sounds like a country in Africa—"

Zeyer cut him off. "What do you want?"

"Well, I could use a few grand." The caller's voice got stronger, sounding more sure of itself. "See, I don't know if you heard, but a woman got herself beaten up pretty bad and drowned here couple of days ago. The word I get is she was wearing a ring like this one. On a silver chain around her neck. The law's saying they'd like this ring pretty bad. 'Course, they won't pay me for it, and there's no way I'll try to sell it retail. That's what got me two years in Millhaven. I figure maybe she had it coming." The caller paused. "Are you gettin' my drift?"

Zeyer looked around again. "Keep talking," he said.

"Now, even if it's not your ring, see, I figure you could give me a couple big ones for it. You could come up here and get it. Then you could fence it in the big city for four, five thousand easy. Double your money, right?"

"You want me to ride all that way on your say-so?"

"Okay, okay. I ain't goin' nowhere else to sell it. So you don't want it, I'll kinda find it all over again. Down under them pines near the shore. Where that girl was beaten up and drowned. I'll give it to the cops and be a hero. They'll track it just like I did and come talkin' to you. If you're cool with that, it's okay with me. I'm not too fond of cops myself, but..."

A long pause.

The caller said, "You still there?"

"I don't know what you're talking about," Zeyer said.

"Well, if that's how you feel..."

"What's your name?"

"I told you. Hank. So you comin' or not?"

"If I want that...that ring," Zeyer said, "and I show up with the cash, what do we do?"

There was a smile in the caller's voice. "Well, see, I'm workin' alone in the back garden today. Nobody's ever around. You come by, you'll see me in a green uniform. Maybe holdin' a rake. Just walk up and introduce yourself. Can you get here by three?

'Cause I'm finished my shift then. I don't want to hold this too long, you know?"

"I'm not saying I know anything about any damn ring," Zeyer said.

"Make it around three, okay? I need to get rid of it one way or the other. If it's not to you, well…" And he hung up.

Martin Zeyer stood with the phone in his hand, thinking. Then he called across to Sparky, "You got my cycle ready?"

Sparky walked toward him, cleaning his hands on a rag. "Had it ready an hour ago. Where you riding to? You pickin' up some stuff?"

"No, nothing like that."

"You're not bringing it in here, right?"

"I'm not picking up anything. I just got to meet a guy. Up north." He forced a smile. "Just an easy ride there and back on a nice day."

• • •

Before leaving, Zeyer stopped at his rented room. From the freezer in his kitchen he took out an opened bag of frozen peas. Beneath the peas were bundles of twenty-dollar bills. He took out a bundle, closed the bag and put it back in the freezer. The money went into an inside pocket of his leather jacket.

He planned to come back with both the money and the ring.

TEN

Most people who visited the Ainslie Inn were into sports. In summer they swam, sailed, golfed and played tennis. In winter they skied and skated. The food was good, and the rooms were cozy.

In summer, much was made of the inn's gardens. Benches and tables were set alongside a rose garden at the back of the inn, facing a large, open lawn. The garden area had been set aside for future use. If the inn were to grow in size, this area would provide space for expansion. Meanwhile, it often sat empty. A wooden shed at the back of the garden served as storage for tools, plant food and equipment.

Martin Zeyer arrived at the Ainslie Inn before three that afternoon. It had been an easy ride north. More than easy—it had been fun. Someday, he thought while he rode, he might buy a place in Muskoka. When he made enough money selling drugs, he could retire there. Then he laughed at his own idea. Retire? Hardly. He was going to raise hell every day of his life.

He parked his cycle in the lot and avoided walking through the lobby. The fewer people who saw him, the better. He walked around the building and entered the garden through the street gate. He stopped to pat the roll of money inside his jacket. Then he strolled through the garden, trying to look interested in flowers and grass.

The only other person in the garden was a man in a green shirt and matching shorts, raking the grass. He wore a straw hat and cheap sunglasses. The guy's a loser, Zeyer said to himself. It's gotta be him.

Zeyer looked from side to side as he approached the man. When he was close enough, he said, "Your name Hank?"

The gardener kept raking and said, without looking up, "Who wants to know?"

Zeyer wanted to punch the skinny old loser in the face and teach him some respect. Instead he said, "I'm a guy looking for jewelry. Know where I can buy some?"

The gardener stopped raking. He rested his hands on top of the rake, looked at Zeyer and then away. Keeping his voice low, he said, "I know where you can get some. For free."

Zeyer forced a smile. "Free's good. Where do I get free jewelry?"

"Well, you see..." The gardener began

raking the lawn again. "You gotta walk to them roses back there." He lifted his head and nodded back toward the inn.

Zeyer waited for the man to say more. When he didn't, Zeyer barked, "I don't want any damn roses!"

"Not gonna get any." The man in the green shirt and shorts kept raking. "You pick them flowers and you're gonna get yourself in trouble. Can't pick flowers around here. Buy 'em at the florist shop inside. That's what you do, you want flowers."

Zeyer stood glaring at the man. Finally he walked closer, so close that the gardener stepped back. Zeyer spoke in a hoarse whisper. "I didn't come for any damn roses. You know what I'm here for. Hand it over or I'll put that rake someplace where it hurts."

The gardener seemed to think about that. Then he said, "You bring the money?"

Zeyer slapped the bulge in his jacket.

"Yeah, I did. So what's this about *free*? What's free? You show me what I want, I give you the cash. I don't even know if you got the thing, right? You show me you got it, I'll give you cash and go."

"I'm just tryin' to prove I'm on the up and up," the gardener said. "We gotta trust each other, right? Am I right? I gotta trust you got the money, and you gotta trust I've got... the thing. The thing you came for." He raised an arm and pointed to the rose garden at the back of the Ainslie Inn. "You go back there to the pink hybrid tea—"

"The what?"

"The pink rosebush in the far corner. Go behind it, see. That's where the chain is. On the shady side. It's yours. That's the first part, right? To prove I got it. The other thing, I mean. What you come for."

"I don't want the chain. You know what I want."

The gardener lowered his voice. "You think I'm gonna hand it over out here?" He looked around, still talking. "And you're gonna hand over all that money out in the open? Where anybody can see us? Listen, my mother, she didn't raise no dummies. Thought you were a smart guy."

Zeyer made a fist. "You're gonna be a *dead* guy if you don't get to the point."

"I'm gettin' there, I'm gettin' there." The gardener bent forward to whisper again. "You get the chain, you know I'm on the level. That's why it's there. To prove it, see? I found 'em together. You get it, you'll know I've got the—" The gardener looked around. "What you come for. Then we can trust each other, right? Am I right?"

When Zeyer said nothing the gardener went on.

"I'll give you what you come for in there." He nodded toward the shed. "Wouldn't expect you to go in there unless you know I'm on the level. See, I'm tryin' to do things right, okay? I know what it's like to stay away from the law, not let 'em catch you at anything." The gardener turned to walk away toward the shed. "I'll be in there waiting. The chain's free. The other thing isn't. So bring the cash."

Zeyer watched the man walk to the shed and enter it. *This guy's smarter than I thought,* he said to himself. *He never mentioned the ring. Anybody listening would have no idea what we're talking about. Sounds like he was telling the truth about having dealt with the law. He must have found the ring and the chain together.*

Zeyer had searched for them in the dark among the pines. He couldn't see his own feet, it was so dark. When the sun came up, they must have been right there in plain sight, the chain and the ring.

Just like Lana was. Out in the water. Sexy, stupid, dead Lana.

Walking back to the rose garden, Zeyer tried again to look like a guest. He stopped to stare up at the inn. Each room had a balcony, and some rooms had hot tubs. Too bad it wasn't him and Lana who had stayed here.

She had it coming. That's what he told himself as he walked. That's what he had been telling himself since it happened. *She had it coming.*

He walked faster as he got closer to the rosebush in the shady corner.

She'd made him do it. If she hadn't tried to make him jealous, she'd still be around. It was her fault. Not his.

His hands were shaking when he reached the garden and stopped, as though admiring the roses. Then he turned to look around him. The garden was as empty as when he had arrived. From the pool on the other side of the resort he heard laughter, splashing and music.

In two strides he was behind the bush, in the shadow of the building. And there it was—the silver chain strung across low branches of the rosebush. Lana had put the ring on that cheap chain after he bought it for her. He'd wanted her to wear it on her finger. *When you tell me you want to marry me,* she had said, *it will go on my finger.*

Yeah? he had said to her. *Well, in that case it'll be around your neck for one hell of a long time.* It had been there for three weeks. He was dumb to buy it just to show her that he could, he thought. And she was even dumber to do and say the things she did.

He knelt to take the chain from the bush and slip it into the pocket of his jeans. He stood and looked around. The garden was still empty. The gardener in his stupid green outfit was going into the shed.

He thought about that. *Who else might be in there with him? Could this be a trap?*

Neither of them had mentioned a ring. It was worth the risk. And the guy had been straight, showing him the chain. He must have the ring. Might have to get a little rough, getting the ring and keeping the cash. But he could handle this loser. *And what could the dude do? Run to the police? Complain about some guy taking a ring that he should have handed over himself?*

No, he won't, Zeyer told himself. *If I have to, I'll give him a couple of slaps on the side of the head and get it for nothing. But he's not getting any money. Not if I can help it.*

He smiled to himself as he walked.

He'd hide the ring and wait a few months. Then he might sell it for five, maybe six grand. He knew a guy who would pay that much.

Or maybe he'd find another sexy Lana. A better one, nice enough that he'd give her the ring. Somebody who wouldn't tease him. Somebody who'd believe he could afford to buy her stuff like that. Somebody who wouldn't run off two weeks later for a weekend with an ex-cop. A dumb cop who just might take the fall for killing her.

Now that would be neat. A cop getting life for something he didn't do.

He started to mount the steps to the door of the garden shed.

Sometimes things work out better than you expect.

He reached for the door and opened it without knocking.

ELEVEN

It took a moment for his eyes to adjust to the dimness. When they did, he saw the gardener sitting behind a table with a deck of cards. Behind him hung several garden tools—rakes, shovels, pitchforks.

Zeyer looked around. Bags of lawn food and fertilizer were stacked against the wall to his left. The wall on the right was covered with charts and calendars. Some were hanging in front of a power lawn mower and a large trash can. One was a poster for a tractor company. It showed a green tractor among giant daisies. *For flowers or forage, this is the one!* the poster said.

Zeyer sniffed the air. The place smelled of dead grass.

"You find what you're looking for?" the gardener said. He was dealing cards on the table. He didn't look up as he spoke.

Zeyer walked to the bags of plant food and weed killer. He looked behind them, making sure they were alone. "Where is it?" he said.

The gardener scooped the cards into a stack and handed it to Zeyer. "You wanna pick a card?" he said.

"Do I want *what*?" Zeyer snarled.

The gardener spread the cards in his hand. "Go ahead. Pick a card. Any card."

"Are you nuts? You know what I came for. Where is it?"

"I've been working on this trick for a week—"

Zeyer slapped the cards from the gardener's hand. They flew through the air and onto the wooden floor. Zeyer's other hand reached across the table and grabbed the man's shirt. "You think you're some kind of clown?" he said. "Well, you'll be a dead clown unless you get me that ring." He pushed the gardener back into his chair.

"Gonna do to me what you did to that woman?" the gardener said. He smoothed the front of his shirt. "The one you killed for the ring?"

"Is that what they think? That I did it to get the ring back?"

"Looked like that to me. Told you, I know diamonds and things. I'm out there the other day, look down, and there's ten, fifteen thousand dollars at my feet. Ring like that, you don't see every day. You didn't come up here for what it's worth, did you? You came for what it could prove. Somebody would know you bought it for her, I'll bet. They found it, they'd be on you like mud on a hog, the cops. Where'd you get that kind of cash anyway?"

Zeyer leaned across the table, coming so close to the gardener that the other man stood and stepped back. "Just so you know, I could've bought ten of those rings. With cash, like I did that one. She said I couldn't afford it. She bugged me so much that I walked in to buy it just to prove I could. And she's not dead because of that ring. It's because she ran off with some guy, used to be a cop. She came up here with him and bragged to me about it. Called me up and told me where she was, said she needed to see me. Wanted me to come up and take her away from the dumb ex-cop. Said she loved me, wanted me to marry her. Asked me to meet her at midnight out in them pine trees.

And call her when I got there. I said sure and that we'd ride off later, back to Toronto. Got her all excited about the idea. I just wanted the ring back. And a chance to teach her not to fool around on me."

"They say she drowned," the gardener said in a low voice. He sounded sad. "They say she was beat up and then held under until she drowned."

"You think I could let her go after smashing her face like I did? I dragged her into the lake so fast, she never had a chance to make a sound. Just a whole bunch of bubbles." Zeyer seemed to realize where he was and what he was saying. He stood back and looked around the room again. "You ever have a woman get to you like that? I'll bet you haven't." He looked at the gold band on the gardener's left hand. "What'd you do? Marry some girl you knocked up in high school? Now you got a bunch of kids and a dead-end job? You can't stand looking at each other, you and her? Is that what happened, loser?"

The gardener looked at the floor. "We don't have children."

"Good for you. Now give me the ring, or you won't have a head either."

"It's outside."

Zeyer looked this way and that. "What's outside?"

"The ring. I'm not going to carry it around on me. I told you, my mother—"

"Yeah, she didn't raise no dummies. Well, one of you better get out there and bring me that ring." He began to walk around the table, his fists clenched.

The gardener reached behind him and seized a pitchfork. He aimed the sharp points at Zeyer and said, "Go get it yourself."

Zeyer took a step back. He considered charging the other man, but the points were sharp. And rusty. Instead he said, "Tell me where it is."

"There's a wooden bin on the far side of the shed," the gardener said. "Full of grass seed. It's in the seed bin out there." He waved his hand to the right. "Out there against the wall. You can feel the ring under the seed. In the top left corner. Get it and get outta here. I don't want the ring, and I don't want your money. Take it and go. Don't ever come back, see?"

Zeyer almost smiled. "I don't ever want to come back here for anything." He walked to the door and turned around. "I got it right here, you know. The money, I mean." He patted his jacket. "But if you don't want it..." He shrugged, opened the door and stepped outside.

The garden was still empty. *Good.* He walked to the corner of the shed and turned to see a large wooden bin against the wall. Just as the loser had said.

Tall pines beside the building kept it in deep shade. The darkness felt cool after the hot sun. It would be good to sit there in the shade, maybe with a cold beer. But he wanted to get on his motorcycle and ride south in the sunshine. With the ring in his pocket.

He wouldn't try to sell the ring after all. Too risky. He would dump it down a sewer somewhere. The loser was right. A piece like that could be traced back to him. Better to dump it. He would write off nearly fifteen thousand dollars to save his skin. But he could afford it. There was another deal coming down next week that would make him two, maybe three times that much money. How many guys could do that?

He walked to the bin and raised the wooden lid.

The bin was almost filled with grass seed. Holding the lid open with one hand, he reached in with his other to the top left corner.

His fingers felt under the seed. There was nothing there. He pushed his hand deeper into the seeds. Still nothing.

Maybe it was in the other corner. He changed hands, using his right hand to look under the seeds, feeling beneath the surface. Nothing there either.

He swore aloud. He should have sent that fool out here to get it himself. He swung his right hand through the seeds in the bin. Now he wasn't feeling beneath the surface. He was flinging seeds out of the bin in handfuls. There was no ring. When he dropped the lid, it landed with a loud thud.

He leaned on the bin to catch his breath and felt his anger rise. He had been taken. By a stupid gardener. One way or another, he would teach that fool a lesson, pitchfork or none. He wiped his hands on his jacket and began walking back to the shed, planning what he would do. There were shovels in that shed. He would grab one and use it. Zeyer had been in enough bar fights to handle himself with some skinny fool. The other guy would have no chance with a pitchfork this time. He would grab a shovel, throw it at the loser, and when he ducked...

Zeyer turned the corner of the shed, and there he was.

The gardener had a smile on his face and a pistol in one hand. In his other hand was a set of handcuffs. "Hi there," he said. "Name's Henry. This here's my boss." He tilted his head at a woman in a police uniform. She was also holding a pistol. "And that there's the manager, Ms Rosart." A tall woman in a gold jacket stood a few steps away, her arms folded.

"Martin Zeyer," the woman in the police uniform said, "you are under arrest for the murder of Lana Jewel Laverne Parker. Turn around and put your hands behind your back."

"You're crazy," Zeyer said.

The woman pulled a Taser from her belt. "You will be on the ground in pain unless you do it," she said.

Zeyer turned around.

"You're gonna be staying with us until the OPP comes for you," Henry said. "Maybe for a couple of hours." The cuffs snapped shut. "That'll be long enough for me to show you a couple of card tricks."

TWELVE

Max sat in a chair, her legs stretched in front of her. She felt both relaxed and excited at the same time. Standing behind her were Margie, Henry and Pam Rosart. Henry was sipping a coffee. Margie punched his shoulder when the video finished. "Boy, you're good," she said. "You could win an Oscar doing that."

"You were right," Henry said to her. "About trying to show him card tricks. Got him so angry he couldn't stop talking to me.

How'd you know it would work?"

Margie just smiled.

Down the hall, Martin Zeyer sat in a cell, his head in his hands.

Max called Sergeant Stanton with the news. "We have the killer of Lana Parker in a cell," she said. "And we have him on video telling what he did and how he did it. I think you need to come and see it."

She did not expect the sergeant to believe her, and he didn't. "You've made a mistake," he said. "We have the man who did it." He meant Jim Benson.

"You need more proof," Max had said. "And you know it."

"We'll find it."

"No, you won't. Because we have it here."

Stanton made a point of sounding bored. "So what is it?"

"Everything you need is on the video, with sound. He brags about what he did and gives us a motive." When Stanton said nothing, she said, "Look, if you or someone from your force doesn't get here soon, I'll pass it on to some TV news outlet."

"You can't do that."

"Why not? You're telling me it's not evidence. So what law would I be breaking?"

She heard Stanton breathe long and hard into the receiver. "If I waste my time coming up there..." he said.

"I'll expect you in an hour," Max said. "Remind me how you take your coffee."

• • •

Stanton was not pleased when he arrived. "If this has been a wild-goose chase," he said, "I will file a report, and from now on you clowns won't be able to do anything more than write parking tickets."

Max ignored his tantrum. "It's in here,"

she said and led him into her office. Henry and Pam Rosart followed them.

It took less than ten minutes to watch the videos. The first showed Zeyer arriving in the garden, approaching Henry and talking to him. Next they watched Zeyer walk back to the rosebush and pull the broken silver chain from its branches. The screen went black.

"Now for act two," Henry said.

The new view showed the inside of the shed. Henry sat to the right, dealing cards on the old table. In a few seconds the door opened and Zeyer entered. Henry looked up and said, *You find what you're looking for?*

They watched and listened as Zeyer bragged about killing Lana Parker. They watched Henry raise the pitchfork to defend himself. When Zeyer left the shed to look for the ring in the seed bin, Henry took his cell phone from a drawer in the table. *He's out*, he said into the phone.

We see him, Max said from inside the inn, where she had been watching through a window. *We're on our way.*

Henry replaced the phone. Then he took his pistol and handcuffs from the drawer and left the shed. Every word and every gesture from Henry and Zeyer was on the video.

"Where did you hide the camera?" Stanton asked. He stared at the screen as though waiting for another show. He looked and sounded weary.

"Behind a tractor poster," Pam Rosart said. "It's one of our portable units. The size of a pack of gum."

Stanton turned to stare at her.

"It's got big flowers on it," Henry said. "The poster, I mean. They're daisies. We cut the center out of one and aimed through the hole. Pretty smart, right?"

Stanton ignored him. "The sound is good," he said. "I could hear every word."

"It will hold up in court," Max said.

Stanton ignored her too. "What got you started on this? What made you think the ring was part of it?"

Instead of answering, Maxine called out, "Margie?"

Margie's gray-haired head peeked around the corner.

"Tell Sergeant Stanton about young men and young women and jewelry," Maxine said.

"My son is a sweetie," Margie said to Stanton. "But when his girl dropped him after he bought her a bracelet—"

Stanton cut her off. "I get the picture."

Margie looked at Maxine, who grinned and shrugged.

"What was all that stuff about numbers on diamonds?" Stanton said. "I've never heard of it."

"Some diamonds are marked with lasers," Max said. "They put a logo on it. We figured they could put numbers on them too."

"Where is the ring?" Stanton said.

Max said, "We don't know."

"You don't know?"

"We never said we had it. Not to you. It may still be out there in the sand. Or maybe it's in the water. Or maybe somebody found it already." She lifted her chin and said, "Does it matter? This is not about a ring. It never was. This is about the murder of a pretty young woman who liked to tease men. She went too far with Zeyer."

Stanton still said nothing. Then, "Do you have a copy?" He meant the video.

Pam Rosart stepped forward. "It's on here," she said. She handed him a memory stick.

"Does this guy Zeyer know he was recorded?" the sergeant asked Max.

She nodded. "We played it for him. Showed it to him through the bars of his cell."

"What did he say?"

"He asked if we would get his motorcycle out of the parking lot. He was afraid somebody would steal it."

"Here's the funny part," Henry said.

Stanton turned to look at him for the first time.

"When we asked where he had parked it, he said it was next to a red Porsche."

"Jim Benson's car." Stanton turned to look back at Max.

"He left it there when you arrested him three days ago," she said. "Now he can come and get it himself, right?"

THIRTEEN

"So that's how it went."

Maxine was sitting on her front patio an hour before sunset. Granite Lake shone like gold in the fading light.

Geegee shook her head and took a sip of wine. "Did this guy Zeyer say any more? After you took him in, I mean?"

Max nodded. She had her own glass of Pinot Grigio, her reward for living through one of the best days of her life. "He talked when he was in the cell. I didn't tell the OPP about it. They might have accused me of interrogating him. We didn't ask him any questions. He just sat in his cell, talking to himself as much as to us. A lot of them do it when they know it's over for them."

"What did he say?"

"Not much we didn't already know or could guess. He said Lana had been his first serious girlfriend, the first one he might have loved. He'd made a drug score and they went downtown to celebrate. They walked past Bentley's, and she saw the ring in the window. When she made a big deal about it, he bragged to her. If she liked it so much, he said, he would buy it for her. She laughed at him, said he couldn't afford it. He got angry and told her he would prove he could."

"Like a little boy," Geegee said, "showing off to some little girl."

Maxine shrugged. "Men are all little

boys around women like her," she said. "He went into the store and asked the price of the ring. Then he told her she would have it the next day."

"He really went back and bought it?"

Maxine nodded. "He paid cash with money from his drug deals. He gave it to her and told her to put it on her finger, but she said not until he proposed to her."

"Do you think he would have?" Geegee poured herself more wine. "Proposed?"

Maxine gave that some thought. "Doubt it. Of course, he might really have been in love with her. As much in love as a guy like that can get."

"Speaking of getting," Geegee said, "what kind of sentence will he get if he is found guilty?"

"His lawyer may tell him to plead guilty to second-degree murder and say he killed her in a rage. He'd probably be right. We can't prove the guy rode up here to kill her."

"So he'd get a shorter sentence?"

"It would still be a life sentence, but with earlier parole." She looked behind her, where the sky had a strange glow. Some people called it the magic hour, but there was nothing magic about what she saw approaching.

Geegee followed her eyes. "Is that..."

Maxine watched the red car pull into her driveway and the driver's door open. The man who stepped out was tall and slim. He wore a light jacket over a denim shirt.

Maxine set her glass aside, stood and walked toward him.

Jim Benson opened his arms to hug her, but Maxine stopped several paces away with her arms folded.

"I have always owed you so much," Jim said. His eyes were dry, but there were tears in his voice. "Now I owe you even more."

Maxine kept her voice steady. "You owe

me nothing. I knew you didn't kill that girl. They had the wrong man, and it was up to me to prove it. That's what I did."

"Yes, you did." Jim leaned against his car. "You were always a great cop. Now you're a great detective."

"All the charges against you are dropped?"

"Free and clear. She played both of us for fools, Zeyer and me. She used me to make him jealous."

"And you jumped at the chance." She turned to walk away. "Of course, you always did."

"Maxine."

She stopped to look back at him. He's at his mellow age, she thought. That's what her mother had said when Maxine's father reached his mid-forties. *Your father is in his mellow age,* she told Maxine. *Mature and sure of himself, yet still young where it matters. I don't think he's ever been sexier.*

Maxine had blushed at her mother's words.

Now she saw the same things in Jim Benson. His hair was gray at the temples, and small crow's-feet spread from the corners of his eyes. His body was still trim and firm. His voice was deep and a little raspy—when he spoke, his words were almost musical. He had mellowed.

She watched him standing in the dying light of the midsummer evening. She saw two things in the same person. A man mellow with age, and a boy in need of a mother.

When he began to speak, she held up a hand. "Nothing has changed," she said. "I want you to go. Get back in your car and go. I'm glad the charges were dropped. That's all. I don't want to hear what you have to say. I just want you to leave. Goodbye."

She turned and walked to pick up her wine. Then she motioned Geegee to follow her inside her home, where she closed and locked the door. She and Geegee watched Jim Benson climb into his car, start the engine and back out of the driveway. They stood listening until all was silent again. Outside, the magic hour was ending. Stars were appearing. There was moonlight on the water. The women returned to the patio and sat back in their chairs.

"Could you hear us?" Maxine said. "Could you hear what we were saying?"

Geegee nodded. She leaned toward Maxine. "Are you all right?"

"I'm fine." Maxine took a sip of wine. "I was pretty abrupt with him."

"Sure you were. But I know why." Maxine looked at Geegee, who said, "You were afraid he would ask if he could come in and stay the evening."

"Not quite." Maxine stared out at the lake. "I was afraid I might be the one who would ask."

The two women sat in silence for a very long time, listening to loons call across the water.

JOHN LAWRENCE REYNOLDS has had more than thirty works of fiction and nonfiction published. His work has earned two Arthur Ellis Awards for Best Mystery Novel, a National Business Book Award and a CBC Bookie Award. His bestselling book *Shadow People*, tracing the development and influence of secret societies through history, was published in fourteen countries and twelve languages. He has also authored several business and investment books, including the bestselling *The Naked Investor* and its sequel, *The Skeptical Investor*, as well as his assessment of the 2008–2009 global financial crisis, *Bubbles, Bankers & Bailouts*. *Murder Among the Pines* is his third book in the Maxine Benson Mystery series, after *A Murder for Max* and *Murder Below Zero*. He lives in Burlington, Ontario, with his wife, Judy. For more information, visit www.wryter.ca.

DON'T MISS THE OTHER
MAXINE BENSON
MYSTERIES!

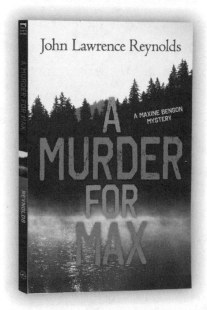

Escaping the pressures of big-city policing,
Maxine Benson is happy to be appointed police
chief in the resort town of Port Ainslie. Max's
biggest challenge is to overcome skepticism at her
ability to deal with major crimes—like the murder
of Billy Ray Edwards. Now Max has to prove
herself to the locals and solve Billy Ray's murder.

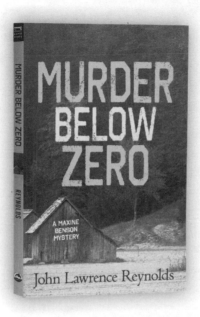

It's almost summer in small town Port Ainslie. Or
is it? Temperatures are so far below normal that
when Police Chief Maxine Benson finds the frozen
body of a man in a ditch, she isn't completely
surprised. Even though Maxine is quickly elbowed
aside by the mostly-male provincial police force,
she can't resist investigating the case on her own.
Will Maxine's skills solve this twisted tale of a case?

ORCA BOOK PUBLISHERS
www.orcabook.com